John 3:16 – A Meditation

The Children's Teacher

Contents

Introduction 1

1. For God… …. 6

2. For God so loved 50

3. For God so loved the world 55

4. For God so loved the world, that he gave 58

5. For God so loved the world, that he gave his only begotten Son 61

6. For God so loved the world, that he gave his only begotten Son, that whosoever believeth in him 75

7. For God so loved the world, that he gave his only begotten Son, that whosoever believeth in him should not perish 81

8. For God so loved the world, that he gave his only begotten Son, that whosoever believeth in him should not perish, but have everlasting life 90

Closing Remarks 97

Introduction

Most Christians make a habit of reading the Bible, but many Christians may never have meditated on Holy Scripture. Many might ask, why meditate on God's word? Consider:

"I will meditate in thy precepts, and have respect unto thy ways."

Psalms 119:15, KJV

"This book of the law shall not depart out of thy mouth; but thou shalt meditate therein day and night, that thou mayest observe to do according to all that is written therein: for then thou shalt make thy way prosperous, and then thou shalt have good success."

Joshua 1:8, KJV

"Meditate upon these things; give thyself wholly to them; that thy profiting may appear to all."

1 Timothy 4:15, KJV

"Blessed is the man that walketh not in the counsel of the ungodly, nor standeth in the way of sinners, nor sitteth in the seat of the scornful.

"But his delight is in the law of the LORD; and in his law doth he meditate day and night."

Psalms 1:1-2, KJV

"MEM. O how love I thy law! It is my meditation all the day.

"Thou through thy commandments hast made me wiser than mine enemies: for they are ever with me.

"I have more understanding than all my teachers: for thy testimonies are my meditation."

Psalms 119:97-99, KJV

The words *meditate and meditation* appear too many times in the Holy Scriptures to just shrug off. We know that God is spirit, and those who seek to worship Him must worship in spirit and in truth, and this includes meditating on the Word of God. Because we are meditating on God's word and not mine, I intend to minimize my words after this introduction and let the Word of God comprise the bulk of our focus.

I pray that as we read (slowly, thoughtfully, carefully) excerpts from Holy Scripture and as we meditate on those passages, the Holy Spirit will guide us into all truth. As we pray to the Lord and read His word, and as we begin to meditate on it, one verse will lead to another, and other verses will come to mind, rising up out of our hearts, out of the Spirit dwelling in our hearts, for our contemplation, and for our enlightenment.

The effect will not be the same for every reader. A verse on the page may bring to one reader's mind one, two, or half a dozen other verses that the Lord wants that reader to linger over, while to another reader's mind, He might bring different verses, and all those verses might be verses that are not contained in these pages, verses that the Lord did not lead me to consider. Our Lord knows each of us – each hair on our heads – and He knows what verses to bring to our minds, and when, and for what purposes.

We meditate on the verses that He brings to mind. We pray that God will open our hearts to the truth in the verses He brings to our attention, and when we take them to heart, He teaches us and changes us. We are doers of the word and not merely hearers. We are not hearing without comprehending. Jesus promised to send the Helper who will lead us into all truth and testify of Him. We have confidence that God will do this. God is pleased to reveal Himself to us; He is a rewarder of those who diligently seek Him. What greater reward can we hope for beyond knowing Him and abiding in Him forever? It is the highest and chief end of man to glorify God and fully to enjoy Him forever. Consider:

"But this shall be the covenant that I will make with the house of Israel; After those days, saith the LORD, I will put my law in their inward parts, and write it in their hearts; and will be their God, and they shall be my people. And they shall teach no more every man his neighbor, and every man his brother, saying Know the LORD: for they shall all know me, from the least of them unto the greatest of them, saith the LORD: for I will forgive their iniquity, and I will remember their sin no more."

Jeremiah 31: 33-34, KJV

"Howbeit when he, the Spirit of truth, is come, he will guide you into all truth: for he shall not speak of himself; but whatsoever he shall hear, that shall he speak: and he will shew you things
to come."

John 16:13, KJV

"John answered and said, A man can receive nothing, except it be given him from heaven. Ye yourselves bear me witness, that I said, I am not the Christ, but that I am sent before him. He that hath the bride is the bridegroom: but the friend of the bridegroom, which standeth and heareth him, rejoiceth greatly because of the bridegroom's voice: this my joy therefore is fulfilled. He must increase, but I must decrease."

John 3:27-30, KJV

We rejoice when we hear the voice of the Lord our God. We rejoice for His law written on the page and in our hearts, for His words, for the guidance of the Holy Spirit into all truth. We rejoice for the illumination given from heaven to us by the Holy Spirit. We rejoice at the words of Jesus being explained to us and revealed to us in our hearts

– not by anything I say, but by the Holy Spirit speaking to us, living inside of us and teaching us, by God Himself leading us to know Him more deeply, more intimately. He is the one leading us to meditate on His word. I must decrease, and He must increase.

So, I am anxious to get this introduction finished so we can really begin to seek to know Him as promised through Jeremiah and as promised through the Lord Jesus Christ.

For forty years, I knew the words of John 3:16. Blessed with God-fearing parents, I had John 3:16 memorized from my pre-school days. But for whatever reason (only God knows), forty years passed before I was led to meditate on the words I had known for so long. I was preparing to teach children at church, and it occurred to me to teach on John 3:16 because we say it together every Wednesday night. Suddenly, the Spirit showed me truth more deeply than I had ever considered it, more deeply than I had ever experienced it, just as our Lord Jesus promised He would.

I was overwhelmed with a flood of verses, a flood of truth. The first six words of the verse resounded deep in my heart as my spirit and His Spirit turned them over and over in my inmost being and pondered them and meditated on them: *For God* – all that He is (can we even begin to scratch the surface of His eternal being! His eternality from our perspective is like the vastness of the cosmos being considered by a speck smaller than a grain of sand; He and all of his attributes are ineffable, too infinitely vast, too infinitely glorious to be expressed or described with words) – *so loved* – real love in the highest sense, not just a bit of affection or flabby sentimentality, but a selfless pouring out of self for the good of another – *the world* – even the most wicked and vile among us, which truly includes all of us; even the most polite and kind among us are like whitewashed tombs, full of filth and decay, for all have sinned and fallen short of the glory of God, and even in that state and condition of lostness, while we were sinners and enemies of God, Christ laid down His life to redeem us.

I was brought to tears. I shook with weeping and felt His Spirit opening the eyes of my understanding. I do not say this to boast; I want everyone in the church to experience what I experienced. I am not suggesting you follow *me*, but that we together follow *Him*. I want this for you, too, for everyone who meditates with the One who calls, chooses, saves, sanctifies, and leads us into all truth. Let us plunge into the depths of deepest profundity together, led by the Holy Spirit to the only begotten Son who is the Way and the Truth and the Life, and by Him to the Father.

May our prayer and purpose echo that of the psalmist who prayed:

"Let the words of my mouth, and the meditation of my heart, be acceptable in thy sight, O LORD, my strength, and my redeemer."

Psalms 19:14, KJV

And let us hear the answering call from above:

"Be still, and know that I am God: I will be exalted among the heathen, I will be exalted in the earth."

Psalms 46:10, KJV

Let us consider:

"For God so loved the world, that he gave his only begotten Son, that whosoever believeth in him should not perish, but have everlasting life."

John 3:16, KJV

1.

For God...

...is SPIRIT

"God is Spirit, and those who worship Him must worship in spirit and truth."

John 4:24, KJV

"And God said unto Moses, I AM THAT I AM: and he said, Thus shalt thou say unto the children of Israel, I AM hath sent me unto you."

Exodus 3:14, KJV

"Thus saith the Lord, The heaven is my throne, and the earth is my footstool: where is the house that ye build unto me? And where is the place of my rest?"

Isaiah 66:1, KJV

For **God…**

…is GOOD

"The LORD is good, a strong hold in the day of trouble; and he knoweth them that trust in him."

Nahum 1:7, KJV

"O give thanks unto the LORD; for he is good; for his mercy endureth for ever."

1 Chronicles 16:34, KJV

"Or despisest thou the riches of his goodness and forbearance and longsuffering; not knowing that the goodness of God leadeth thee to repentance?"

Romans 2:4, KJV

"The LORD is good unto them that wait for him, to the soul that seeketh him."

Lamentations 3:25, KJV

"If ye then, being evil, know how to give good gifts unto your children, how much more shall your Father which is in heaven give good things to them that ask him?"

Matthew 7:11, KJV

For **God…**

   …is GOOD

"Every good gift and every perfect gift is from above, and cometh down from the Father of lights, with whom is no variableness, neither shadow of turning."

James 1:17, KJV

"But I say unto you, Love your enemies, bless them that curse you, do good to them that hate you, and pray for them which despitefully use you, and persecute you;

"That ye may be the children of your Father which is in heaven: for he maketh his sun to rise on the evil and on the good, and sendeth rain on the just and on the unjust."

Matthew 5:44-45, KJV

For **God…**

…is PERFECT AND HOLY

"In the year that king Uzziah died I saw also the Lord sitting upon a throne, high and lifted up, and his train filled the temple.

"Above it stood the seraphims: each one had six wings; with twain he covered his face, and with twain he covered his feet, and with twain he did fly.

"And one cried unto another, and said, Holy, holy, holy, is the LORD of hosts: the whole earth is full of his glory."

Isaiah 6:1-3, KJV

"But as he which hath called you is holy, so be ye holy in all manner of conversation;

"Because it is written, Be ye holy; for I am holy."

1 Peter 1:15-16, KJV

"Be ye therefore perfect, even as your Father which is in heaven is perfect."

Matthew 5:48, KJV

"For thus saith the high and lofty One that inhabiteth eternity, whose name is Holy; I dwell in the high and holy place, with him also that is of a contrite and humble spirit, to revive the spirit of the humble, and to revive the heart of the contrite ones."

Isaiah 57:15, KJV

For **God…**

…is PERFECT AND HOLY

"There is none holy as the LORD: for there is none beside thee: neither is there any rock like our God."

1 Samuel 2:2, KJV

"And when the LORD saw that he turned aside to see, God called unto him out of the midst of the bush, and said, Moses, Moses. And he said, Here am I.

"And he said, Draw not nigh hither: put off thy shoes from off thy feet, for the place whereon thou standest is holy ground."

Exodus 2:4-5, KJV

For **God…**

…is IMMUTABLE

"For I am the Lord, I change not; therefore ye sons of Jacob are not consumed."

Malachi 3:6, KJV

"And God said unto Moses, I AM THAT I AM: and he said, Thus shalt thou say unto the children of Israel, I AM hath sent me unto you."

Exodus 3:14, KJV

"Wherein God, willing more abundantly to shew unto the heirs of promise the immutability of his counsel, confirmed it by an oath:"

Hebrews 6:17, KJV

"Every good gift and every perfect gift is from above, and cometh down from the Father of lights, with whom is no variableness, neither shadow of turning."

James 1:17, KJV

For **God...**

      ...is CREATOR

"Thou art worthy, O Lord, to receive glory and honour and power: for thou hast created all things, and for thy pleasure they are and were created."

Revelation 4:11, KJV

"In the beginning was the Word, and the Word was with God, and the Word was God.

"The same was in the beginning with God.

"All things were made by him; and without him was not any thing made that was made."

John 1:1-3, KJV

"Thus saith the LORD, The heaven is my throne, and the earth is my footstool: where is the house that ye build unto me? and where is the place of my rest?

"For all those things hath mine hand made, and all those things have been, saith the LORD: but to this man will I look, even to him that is poor and of a contrite spirit, and trembleth at my word."

Isaiah 66:1-2, KJV

"In the beginning God created the heaven and the earth."

Genesis 1:1, KJV

For God...

...is CREATOR

"For of him, and through him, and to him, are all things: to whom be glory for ever. Amen."

Romans 11:36, KJV

For **God…**

…is ETERNAL

"And the four beasts had each of them six wings about him; and they were full of eyes within: and they rest not day and night, saying, Holy, holy, holy, Lord God Almighty, which was, and is, and is to come."

Revelation 4:8, KJV

"I am Alpha and Omega, the beginning and the end, the first and the last."

Revelation 22:13, KJV

"And God said unto Moses, I AM THAT I AM: and he said, Thus shalt thou say unto the children of Israel, I AM hath sent me unto you."

Exodus 3:14, KJV

"For thus saith the high and lofty One that inhabiteth eternity, whose name is Holy; I dwell in the high and holy place, with him also that is of a contrite and humble spirit, to revive the spirit of the humble, and to revive the heart of the contrite ones."

Isaiah 57:15, KJV

For **God...**

...is SELF-SUFFICIENT

"For who hath known the mind of the Lord? or who hath been his counsellor?

"Or who hath first given to him, and it shall be recompensed unto him again?"

Romans 11:34-35, KJV

"Then the LORD answered Job out of the whirlwind, and said,

"Who is this that darkeneth counsel by words without knowledge?

"Gird up now thy loins like a man; for I will demand of thee, and answer thou me.

"Where wast thou when I laid the foundations of the earth? declare, if thou hast understanding.

"Who hath laid the measures thereof, if thou knowest? or who hath stretched the line upon it?

"Whereupon are the foundations thereof fastened? or who laid the corner stone thereof;

"When the morning stars sang together, and all the sons of God shouted for joy?"

Job 38:1-7, KJV

"And God said unto Moses, I AM THAT I AM: and he said, Thus shalt thou say unto the children of Israel, I AM hath sent me unto you."

Exodus 3:14, KJV

For **God…**

    …is OMNIPRESENT

"Whither shall I go from thy spirit? or whither shall I flee from thy presence?

"If I ascend up into heaven, thou art there: if I make my bed in hell, behold, thou art there.

"If I take the wings of the morning, and dwell in the uttermost parts of the sea;

"Even there shall thy hand lead me, and thy right hand shall hold me."

Psalms 139: 7-10, KJV

"For where two or three are gathered together in my name, there am I in the midst of them."

Matthew 18:20, KJV

"Thus saith the Lord, The heaven is my throne, and the earth is my footstool: where is the house that ye build unto me? And where is the place of my rest?"

Isaiah 66:1, KJV

"That Christ may dwell in your hearts by faith; that ye, being rooted and grounded in love,

"May be able to comprehend with all saints what is the breadth, and length, and depth, and height;

For **God...**

...is OMNIPRESENT

(cont.) "And to know the love of Christ, which passeth knowledge, that ye might be filled with all the fulness of God."

Ephesians 3:17-19, KJV

For **God…**

...is OMNISCIENT AND WISE

"O the depth of the riches both of the wisdom and knowledge of God! how unsearchable are his judgments, and his ways past finding out!

"For who hath known the mind of the Lord? or who hath been his counsellor?"

Romans 11:33-34, KJV

"Shall not God search this out? for he knoweth the secrets of the heart."

Psalms 44:21, KJV

"But the LORD said unto Samuel, Look not on his countenance, or on the height of his stature; because I have refused him: for the LORD seeth not as man seeth; for man looketh on the outward appearance, but the LORD looketh on the heart."

1 Samuel 16:7, KJV

"And, behold, certain of the scribes said within themselves, This man blasphemeth.

"And Jesus knowing their thoughts said, Wherefore think ye evil in your hearts?"

Matthew 9:3-4, KJV

For **God…**

…is OMNISCIENT AND WISE

"Then there arose a reasoning among them, which of them should be greatest.

"And Jesus, perceiving the thought of their heart, took a child, and set him by him,

"And said unto them, Whosoever shall receive this child in my name receiveth me: and whosoever shall receive me receiveth him that sent me: for he that is least among you all, the same shall be great."

Luke 9:46-48, KJV

For **God…**

…is OMNIPOTENT

"And I heard as it were the voice of a great multitude, and as the voice of many waters, and as the voice of mighty thunderings, saying, Alleluia: for the Lord God omnipotent reigneth."

Revelation 19:6, KJV

"Trust ye in the LORD for ever: for in the LORD JEHOVAH is everlasting strength:

"For he bringeth down them that dwell on high; the lofty city, he layeth it low; he layeth it low, even to the ground; he bringeth it even to the dust."

Isaiah 26:4-5, KJV

"According as his divine power hath given unto us all things that pertain unto life and godliness, through the knowledge of him that hath called us to glory and virtue"

2 Peter 1:3, KJV

"Behold, I am the LORD, the God of all flesh: is there any thing too hard for me?"

Jeremiah 32:27, KJV

For **God...**

   ...is FATHER

"Doubtless thou art our father, though Abraham be ignorant of us, and Israel acknowledge us not: thou O LORD, art our father, our redeemer; they name is from everlasting."

Isaiah 63:16, KJV

"For ye have not received the spirit of bondage again to fear; but ye have received the Spirit of adoption, whereby we cry, Abba, Father."

Romans 8:15, KJV

"But thou, when thou prayest, enter into thy closet, and when thou has shut thy door, pray to thy Father which is in secret; and thy Father which seeth in secret shall reward thee openly.

"But when ye pray, use not vain repetitions, as the heathen do: for they think that they shall be heard for their much speaking.

"Be ye not like unto them: for your Father knoweth what things ye have need of, before ye ask him.

"After this manner therefore pray ye: Our Father which art in heaven, Hallowed be thy name.

"Thy kingdom come. Thy will be done in earth, as it is in heaven.

"Give us this day our daily bread.

"And forgive us our debts, as we forgive our debtors.

"And lead us not into temptation, but deliver us from evil: For thine is the kingdom, and the power, and the glory, for ever. Amen.

For **God…**

 …is FATHER

(cont.) "For if ye forgive not men their trespasses, neither will your Father forgive your trespasses."

Matthew 6:6-9, KJV

"And he said, A certain man had two sons:

"And the younger of them said to his father, Father, give me the portion of goods that falleth to me. And he divided unto them his living.

"And not many days after the younger son gathered all together, and took his journey into a far country, and there wasted his substance with riotous living.

"And when he had spent all, there arose a mighty famine in that land; and he began to be in want.

"And he went and joined himself to a citizen of that country; and he sent him into his fields to feed swine.

"And he would fain have filled his belly with the husks that the swine did eat: and no man gave unto him.

"And when he came to himself, he said, How many hired servants of my father's have bread enough and to spare, and I perish with hunger!

"I will arise and go to my father, and will say unto him, Father, I have sinned against heaven, and before thee,

"And am no more worthy to be called thy son: make me as one of thy hired servants.

For **God**...

...is FATHER

(cont.) "And he arose, and came to his father. But when he was yet a great way off, his father saw him, and had compassion, and ran, and fell on his neck, and kissed him.

"And the son said unto him, Father, I have sinned against heaven, and in thy sight, and am no more worthy to be called thy son.

"But the father said to his servants, Bring forth the best robe, and put it on him; and put a ring on his hand, and shoes on his feet:

"And bring hither the fatted calf, and kill it; and let us eat, and be merry:

"For this my son was dead, and is alive again; he was lost, and is found. And they began to be merry."

Luke 15:11-24, KJV

For **God...**

...is GENEROUS

"But I say unto you, Love your enemies, bless them that curse you, do good to them that hate you, and pray for them which despitefully use you, and persecute you;

"That ye may be the children of your Father which is in heaven: for he maketh his sun to rise on the evil and on the good, and sendeth rain on the just and on the unjust."

Matthew 5:44-45, KJV

"And the LORD spake unto Moses, saying,

"I have heard the murmurings of the children of Israel: speak unto them, saying, At even ye shall eat flesh, and in the morning ye shall be filled with bread; and ye shall know that I am the LORD your God.

"And it came to pass, that at even the quails came up, and covered the camp: and in the morning the dew lay round about the host.

"And when the dew that lay was gone up, behold, upon the face of the wilderness there lay a small round thing, as small as the hoar frost on the ground.

"And when the children of Israel saw it, they said one to another, it is manna: for they wist not what it was. And Moses said unto them, This is the bread which the LORD hath given you to eat....

"And the children of Israel did eat manna forty years, until they came to a land inhabited; they did eat manna, until they came unto the borders of the land of Canaan."

Exodus 16:11-14, 35

For **God…**

…is MERCIFUL AND FORGIVING

"Be ye therefore merciful, as your Father also is merciful."

Luke 6:36, KJV

"But God, who is rich in mercy, for his great love wherewith he loved us,

"Even when we were dead in sins, hath quickened us together with Christ, (by grace ye are saved;)"

Ephesians 2:4-5, KJV

"O give thanks unto the LORD, for he is good: for his mercy endureth for ever."

Psalms 107:1

"And God saw their works, that they turned from their evil way; and God repented of the evil, that he had said that he would do unto them; and he did it not."

Jonah 3:10, KJV

"And the LORD repented of the evil which he thought to do unto his people."

Exodus 32:14, KJV

25

For **God…**

…is MERCIFUL AND FORGIVING

"For when we were yet without strength, in due time Christ died for the ungodly. For scarcely for a righteous man will one die: yet peradventure for a good man some would even dare to die. But God commendeth his love toward us, in that, while we were yet sinners, Christ died for us."

Romans 5:6-8, KJV

"It is of the LORD'S mercies that we are not consumed, because his compassions fail not. They are new every morning: great is thy faithfulness."

Lamentations 3:22-23, KJV

"Nevertheless for thy great mercies' sake thou didst not utterly consume them, nor forsake them; for thou art a gracious and merciful God."

Nehemiah 9:31, KJV

"And he spake this parable unto them, saying,

"What man of you, having a hundred sheep, if he lose one of them, doth not leave the ninety and nine in the wilderness, and go after that which is lost, until he find it?

"And when he hath found it, he layeth it on his shoulders, rejoicing.

"And when he cometh home, he calleth together his friends and neighbours, saying unto them, Rejoice with me; for I have found my sheep which was lost.

For **God...**

...is MERCIFUL AND FORGIVING

(cont.) "I say unto you, that likewise joy shall be in heaven over one sinner that repenteth, more than over ninety and nine just persons, which need no repentance."

Luke 15:3-7, KJV

"For he saith to Moses, I will have mercy on whom I will have mercy, and I will have compassion on whom I will have compassion.

"So then it is not of him that willeth, nor of him that runneth, but of God that sheweth mercy."

Romans 9:15-16, KJV

"The LORD is merciful and gracious, slow to anger, and plenteous in mercy.

"He will not always chide: neither will he keep his anger for ever.

"He hath not dealt with us after our sins; nor rewarded us according to our iniquities.

"For as the heaven is high above the earth, so great is his mercy toward them that fear him."

Psalms 103:8-11, KJV

"But though he cause grief, yet will he have compassion according to the multitude of his mercies."

Lamentations 3:32, KJV

For **God…**

...is MERCIFUL AND FORGIVING

"To the Lord our God belong mercies and forgivenesses, though we have rebelled against him;"

Daniel 9:9, KJV

"Great are thy tender mercies, O LORD; quicken me according to thy judgments."

Psalms 119:156, KJV

For **God…**

…is FAITHFUL

"It is of the LORD'S mercies that we are not consumed, because his compassions fail not. They are new every morning: great is thy faithfulness."

Lamentations 3:22-23, KJV

"If we believe not, yet he abideth faithful: he cannot deny himself."

2 Timothy 2:13, KJV

"LAMED. For ever, O LORD, thy word is settled in heaven.

"Thy faithfulness is unto all generations: thou hast established the earth, and it abideth."

Psalms 119:89-90, KJV

"If we confess our sins, he is faithful and just to forgive us our sins, and to cleanse us from all unrighteousness."

1 John 1:9, KJV

For **God...**

     ...is GRACIOUS

"For by grace are ye saved through faith; and that not of yourselves: it is the gift of God:

"Not of works, lest any man should boast."

Ephesians 2:8-9, KJV

"And he said, I will make all my goodness pass before thee, and I will proclaim the name of the LORD before thee; and will be gracious to whom I will be gracious, and will shew mercy on whom I will shew mercy."

Exodus 33:19, KJV

"Gracious is the LORD, and righteous; yea, our God is merciful."

Psalms 116:5, KJV

"And rend your heart, and not your garments, and turn unto the LORD your God: for he is gracious and merciful, slow to anger, and of great kindness, and repenteth him of the evil."

Joel 2:13, KJV

"For if ye turn again unto the LORD, your brethren and your children shall find compassion before them that lead them captive, so that they shall come again into this land: for the LORD your God is gracious and merciful, and will not turn away his face from you, if ye return unto him."

2 Chronicles 30:9, KJV

For **God…**

…is PATIENT

"Or despisest thou the riches of his goodness and forbearance and longsuffering; not knowing that the goodness of God leadeth thee to repentance?"

Romans 2:4, KJV

"The Lord is not slack concerning his promise, as some men count slackness; but is longsuffering to us-ward, not willing that any should perish, but that all should come to repentance."

2 Peter 3:9, KJV

"The LORD is gracious, and full of compassion; slow to anger, and of great mercy."

Psalms 145:8, KJV

"And account that the longsuffering of our Lord is salvation; even as our beloved brother Paul also according to the wisdom given unto him hath written unto you."

2 Peter 3:15, KJV

"And therefore will the LORD wait, that he may be gracious unto you, and therefore will he be exalted, that he may have mercy upon you: for the LORD is a God of judgment: blessed are all they that wait for him."

Isaiah 30:18, KJV

For **God…**

   …is JUDGE

"For the LORD is our judge, the LORD is our lawgiver, the LORD is our king; he will save us." Isaiah 33:22, KJV

"But God is the judge: he putteth down one, and setteth up another."

Psalms 75:7, KJV

"Henceforth there is laid up for me a crown of righteousness, which the Lord, the righteous judge, shall give me at that day: and not to me only, but unto all them also that love his appearing."

2 Timothy 4:8, KJV

"And thinkest thou this, O man, that judgest them which do such things, and doest the same, that thou shalt escape the judgment of God?"

Romans 2:3, KJV

"And after these things I heard a great voice of much people in heaven, saying, Alleluia; Salvation, and glory, and honour, and power, unto the Lord our God:

"For true and righteous are his judgments: for he hath judged the great whore, which did corrupt the earth with her fornication, and hath avenged the blood of his servants at her hand."

Revelation 19:1-2, KJV

For **God…**

…is JUDGE

"The Lord knoweth how to deliver the godly out of temptations, and to reserve the unjust unto the day of judgment to be punished."

2 Peter 2:9, KJV

"I the LORD search the heart, I try the reins, even to give every man according to his ways, and according to the fruit of his doings."

Jeremiah 17:10, KJV

"And I saw the dead, small and great, stand before God; and the books were opened: and another book was opened, which is the book of life: and the dead were judged out of those things which were written in the books, according to their works."

Revelation 20:12, KJV

"For we know him that hath said, Vengeance belongeth unto me, I will recompense, saith the Lord. And again, The Lord shall judge his people.

"It is a fearful thing to fall into the hands of the living God."

Hebrews 10:30-31, KJV

For **God…**

…is JUDGE

"And I will come near to you to judgment; and I will be a swift witness against the sorcerers, and against the adulterers, and against false swearers, and against those that oppress the hireling in his wages, the widow, and the fatherless, and that turn aside the stranger from his right, and fear not me, saith the LORD of hosts."

Malachi 3:5, KJV

For **God...**

...is SOVEREIGN

"Thou shalt bring them in, and plant them in the mountain of thine inheritance, in the place, O LORD, which thou hast made for thee to dwell in, in the Sanctuary, O Lord, which thy hands have established.

"The LORD shall reign for ever and ever."

Exodus 15:17-18, KJV

"The LORD shall reign for ever, even thy God, O Zion, unto all generations. Praise ye the LORD."

Psalms 146:10, KJV

"And why call ye me, Lord, Lord, and do not the things which I say?"

Luke 6:46, KJV

"And the seventh angel sounded; and there were great voices in heaven, saying, The kingdoms of this world are become the kingdoms of our Lord, and of his Christ; and he shall reign for ever and ever.

"And the four and twenty elders, which sat before God on their seats, fell upon their faces, and worshipped God,

"Saying, We give thee thanks, O Lord God Almighty, which art, and wast, and art to come; because thou hast taken to thee thy great power, and hast reigned."

Revelation 11:15-17, KJV

For **God…**

    …is SOVEREIGN

"And I heard a great voice out of heaven saying, Behold, the tabernacle of God is with men, and he will dwell with them, and they shall be his people, and God himself shall be with them, and be their God."

Revelation 21:3, KJV

"And not only this; but when Rebecca also had conceived by one, even by our father Isaac;

"(For the children being not yet born, neither having done any good or evil, that the purpose of God according to election might stand, not of works, but of him that calleth;)

"It was said unto her, The elder shall serve the younger.

"As it is written, Jacob have I loved, but Esau have I hated.

"What shall we say then? Is there unrighteousness with God? God forbid.

"For he saith to Moses, I will have mercy on whom I will have mercy, and I will have compassion on whom I will have compassion.

"So then it is not of him that willeth, nor of him that runneth, but of God that sheweth mercy.

"For the scripture saith unto Pharaoh, Even for this same purpose have I raised thee up, that I might shew my power in thee, and that my name might be declared throughout all the earth.

"Therefore hath he mercy on whom he will have mercy, and whom he will he hardeneth.

"Thou wilt say then unto me, Why doth he yet find fault? For who hath resisted his will?

(cont.) "Nay but, O man, who art thou that repliest against God? Shall the thing formed say to him that formed it, Why hast thou made me thus?

"Hath not the potter power over the clay, of the same lump to make one vessel unto honour, and another unto dishonour?

"What if God, willing to shew his wrath, and to make his power known, endured with much longsuffering the vessels of wrath fitted to destruction:

"And that he might make known the riches of his glory on the vessels of mercy, which he had afore prepared unto glory,

"Even us, whom he hath called, not of the Jews only, but also of the Gentiles?"

Romans 9:10-24, KJV

"Thou shalt have no other gods before me."

Exodus 20:3, KJV

"O the depth of the riches both of the wisdom and knowledge of God! how unsearchable are his judgments, and his ways past finding out!

"For who hath known the mind of the Lord? or who hath been his counsellor?

"Or who hath first given to him, and it shall be recompensed unto him again?

"For of him, and through him, and to him, are all things: to whom be glory for ever. Amen."

Romans 11:33-36, KJV

For **God...**

    ...is SOVEREIGN

"Then the LORD answered Job out of the whirlwind, and said,

"Who is this that darkeneth counsel by words without knowledge?

"Gird up now thy loins like a man; for I will demand of thee, and answer thou me.

"Where wast thou when I laid the foundations of the earth? declare, if thou hast understanding.

"Who hath laid the measures thereof, if thou knowest? or who hath stretched the line upon it?

"Whereupon are the foundations thereof fastened? or who laid the corner stone thereof;

"When the morning stars sang together, and all the sons of God shouted for joy?

"Or who shut up the sea with doors, when it brake forth, as if it had issued out of the womb?

"When I made the cloud the garment thereof, and thick darkness a swaddlingband for it,

"And brake up for it my decreed place, and set bars and doors,

"And said, Hitherto shalt thou come, but no further: and here shall thy proud waves be stayed?

"Hast thou commanded the morning since thy days; and caused the dayspring to know his place;

"That it might take hold of the ends of the earth, that the wicked might be shaken out of it?"

For **God...**

...is SOVEREIGN

(cont.) "It is turned as clay to the seal; and they stand as a garment.

"And from the wicked their light is withholden, and the high arm shall be broken.

"Hast thou entered into the springs of the sea? or hast thou walked in the search of the depth?

"Have the gates of death been opened unto thee? or hast thou seen the doors of the shadow of death?

"Hast thou perceived the breadth of the earth? declare if thou knowest it all.

"Where is the way where light dwelleth? and as for darkness, where is the place thereof,

"That thou shouldest take it to the bound thereof, and that thou shouldest know the paths to the house thereof?

"Knowest thou it, because thou wast then born? or because the number of thy days is great?

"Hast thou entered into the treasures of the snow? or hast thou seen the treasures of the hail,

"Which I have reserved against the time of trouble, against the day of battle and war?

"By what way is the light parted, which scattereth the east wind upon the earth?

"Who hath divided a watercourse for the overflowing of waters, or a way for the lightning of thunder;

For **God...**

...is SOVEREIGN

(cont.) "To cause it to rain on the earth, where no man is; on the wilderness, wherein there is no man;

"To satisfy the desolate and waste ground; and to cause the bud of the tender herb to spring forth?

"Hath the rain a father? or who hath begotten the drops of dew?

"Out of whose womb came the ice? and the hoary frost of heaven, who hath gendered it?

 "The waters are hid as with a stone, and the face of the deep is frozen.

"Canst thou bind the sweet influences of Pleiades, or loose the bands of Orion?

"Canst thou bring forth Mazzaroth in his season? or canst thou guide Arcturus with his sons?

"Knowest thou the ordinances of heaven? canst thou set the dominion thereof in the earth?

"Canst thou lift up thy voice to the clouds, that abundance of waters may cover thee?

"Canst thou send lightnings, that they may go, and say unto thee, Here we are?

"Who hath put wisdom in the inward parts? or who hath given understanding to the heart?

Job 38:1-36

For **God…**

…is SOVEREIGN

"Are not two sparrows sold for a farthing? and one of them shall not fall on the ground without your Father."

Matthew 10:29, KJV

"And when the LORD saw that he turned aside to see, God called unto him out of the midst of the bush, and said, Moses, Moses. And he said, Here am I.

"And he said, Draw not nigh hither: put off thy shoes from off thy feet, for the place whereon thou standest is holy ground."

Exodus 2:4-5, KJV

"For the LORD is our judge, the LORD is our lawgiver, the LORD is our king; he will save us." Isaiah 33:22, KJV

"And God spake all these words, saying,

"I am the LORD thy God, which have brought thee out of the land of Egypt, out of the house of bondage.

"Thou shalt have no other gods before me."

Exodus 20:1-3, KJV

For **God...**

...is SOVEREIGN

"Hear, O Israel: The LORD our God is one LORD:

"And thou shalt love the LORD thy God with all thine heart, and with all thy soul, and with all thy might."

Deuteronomy 6:4-5, KJV

For **God…**

    …is GLORIOUS

"In the year that king Uzziah died I saw also the Lord sitting upon a throne, high and lifted up, and his train filled the temple.

"Above it stood the seraphims: each one had six wings; with twain he covered his face, and with twain he covered his feet, and with twain he did fly.

"And one cried unto another, and said, Holy, holy, holy, is the LORD of hosts: the whole earth is full of his glory."

Isaiah 6:1-3, KJV

"Who is this King of glory? The LORD of hosts, he is the King of glory. Selah."

Psalms 24:10, KJV

"For of him, and through him, and to him, are all things: to whom be glory for ever. Amen."

Romans 11:36, KJV

"Now therefore, our God, we thank thee, and praise thy glorious name."

1 Chronicles 29:13, KJV

For **God**…

    …is GLORIOUS

"Let them praise the name of the LORD: for his name alone is excellent; his glory is above the earth and heaven."

Psalms 148:13, KJV

"Be thou exalted, O God, above the heavens: and thy glory above all the earth;"

Psalms 108:5, KJV

For **God…**

…is LIGHT

"This then is the message which we have heard of him, and declare unto you, that God is light, and in him is no darkness at all."

1 John 1:5, KJV

"Every good gift and every perfect gift is from above, and cometh down from the Father of lights, with whom is no variableness, neither shadow of turning."

James 1:17, KJV

"For God, who commanded the light to shine out of darkness, hath shined in our hearts, to give the light of the knowledge of the glory of God in the face of Jesus Christ."

2 Corinthians 4:6, KJV

"In him was life; and the life was the light of men.

"And the light shineth in darkness; and the darkness comprehended it not."

John 1:4-5

For **God…**

    …is LIGHT

"And this is the condemnation, that light is come into the world, and men loved darkness rather than light, because their deeds were evil.

"For every one that doeth evil hateth the light, neither cometh to the light, lest his deeds should be reproved.

"But he that doeth truth cometh to the light, that his deeds may be made manifest, that they are wrought in God."

John 3:19-21

"For with thee is the fountain of life: in thy light shall we see light."

Psalms 36:9, KJV

"The people that walked in darkness have seen a great light: they that dwell in the land of the shadow of death, upon them hath the light shined."

Isaiah 9:2, KJV

For **God…**

…is LIGHT

"That thou keep this commandment without spot, unrebukeable, until the appearing of our Lord Jesus Christ:

"Which in his times he shall shew, who is the blessed and only Potentate, the King of kings, and Lord of lords;

"Who only hath immortality, dwelling in the light which no man can approach unto; whom no man hath seen, nor can see: to whom be honour and power everlasting. Amen."

1 Timothy 6:14-16, KJV

"Then spake Jesus again unto them, saying, I am the light of the world: he that followeth me shall not walk in darkness, but shall have the light of life."

John 8:12, KJV

For **God…**

    …is LOVE

"He that loveth not knoweth not God; for God is love."

1 John 4:8, KJV

"How excellent is thy lovingkindness, O God! therefore the children of men put their trust under the shadow of thy wings."

Psalms 36:7, KJV

"For I, saith the LORD, will be unto her a wall of fire round about, and will be the glory in the midst of her.

"For thus saith the LORD of hosts; After the glory hath he sent me unto the nations which spoiled you: for he that toucheth you toucheth the apple of his eye."

Zechariah 2:4, 8

"I have loved you, saith the LORD. Yet ye say, Wherein hast thou loved us? Was not Esau Jacob's brother? saith the LORD: yet I loved Jacob,"

Malachi 1:2, KJV

"But love ye your enemies, and do good, and lend, hoping for nothing again; and your reward shall be great, and ye shall be the children of the Highest: for he is kind unto the unthankful and to the evil."

Luke 6:35, KJV

For **God…**

…is LOVE

"The LORD thy God in the midst of thee is mighty; he will save, he will rejoice over thee with joy; he will rest in his love, he will joy over thee with singing."

Zephaniah 3:17, KJV

"Are not two sparrows sold for a farthing? and one of them shall not fall on the ground without your Father.

"But the very hairs of your head are all numbered.

"Fear ye not therefore, ye are of more value than many sparrows."

Matthew 10:29-31, KJV

"But God commendeth his love toward us, in that, while we were yet sinners, Christ died for us."

Romans 5:8, KJV

"And to know the love of Christ, which passeth knowledge, that ye might be filled with all the fulness of God."

Ephesians 3:19, KJV

2.

For God so loved

"He that loveth not knoweth not God; for God is love. In this was manifested the love of God toward us, because that God sent his only begotten Son into the world, that we might live through him. Herein is love, not that we loved God, but that he loved us, and sent his Son to be the propitiation for our sins."

1 John 4:8-10, KJV

"Ye have heard that it hath been said, Thou shalt love thy neighbour, and hate thine enemy. But I say unto you, Love your enemies, bless them that curse you, do good to them that hate you, and pray for them which despitefully use you, and persecute you; That ye may be the children of your Father which is in heaven: for he maketh his sun to rise on the evil and on the good, and sendeth rain on the just and on the unjust."

Matthew 5:44-45, KJV

"I have loved you, saith the LORD. Yet ye say, Wherein hast thou loved us? Was not Esau Jacob's brother? saith the LORD: yet I loved Jacob,"

Malachi 1:2, KJV

"I will heal their backsliding, I will love them freely: for mine anger is turned away from him."

Hosea 14:4, KJV

For God **so loved…**

"And hope maketh not ashamed; because the love of God is shed abroad in our hearts by the Holy Ghost which is given unto us."

Romans 5:5, KJV

"The LORD hath appeared of old unto me, saying, Yea, I have loved thee with an everlasting love: therefore with lovingkindness have I drawn thee."

Jeremiah 31:3, KJV

"And he arose, and came to his father. But when he was yet a great way off, his father saw him, and had compassion, and ran, and fell on his neck, and kissed him.

"And the son said unto him, Father, I have sinned against heaven, and in thy sight, and am no more worthy to be called thy son.

"But the father said to his servants, Bring forth the best robe, and put it on him; and put a ring on his hand, and shoes on his feet:

"And bring hither the fatted calf, and kill it; and let us eat, and be merry:

"For this my son was dead, and is alive again; he was lost, and is found. And they began to be merry."

Luke 15:20-24, KJV

"He that hath my commandments, and keepeth them, he it is that loveth me: and he that loveth me shall be loved of my Father, and I will love him, and will manifest myself to him."

John 14:21, KJV

For God **so loved…**

"Moreover he said, I am the God of thy father, the God of Abraham, the God of Isaac, and the God of Jacob. And Moses hid his face; for he was afraid to look upon God.

"And the LORD said, I have surely seen the affliction of my people which are in Egypt, and have heard their cry by reason of their taskmasters; for I know their sorrows;

"And I am come down to deliver them out of the hand of the Egyptians, and to bring them up out of that land unto a good land and a large, unto a land flowing with milk and honey"

Exodus 3:6-8a, KJV

"Charity suffereth long, and is kind; charity envieth not; charity vaunteth not itself, is not puffed up, Doth not behave itself unseemly, seeketh not her own, is not easily provoked, thinketh no evil; Rejoiceth not in iniquity, but rejoiceth in the truth;"

1 Corinthians 13:4-6, KJV

"Behold, the days come, saith the LORD, that I will make a new covenant with the house of Israel, and with the house of Judah:

"Not according to the covenant that I made with their fathers in the day that I took them by the hand to bring them out of the land of Egypt; which my covenant they brake, although I was an husband unto them, saith the LORD:"

Jeremiah 31:31-32, KJV

For God **so loved...**

"I am the rose of Sharon, and the lily of the valleys.

"As the lily among thorns, so is my love among the daughters.

"As the apple tree among the trees of the wood, so is my beloved among the sons. I sat down under his shadow with great delight, and his fruit was sweet to my taste.

"He brought me to the banqueting house, and his banner over me was love."

Song of Solomon 2:1-4, KJV

"But when he saw the multitudes, he was moved with compassion on them, because they fainted, and were scattered abroad, as sheep having no shepherd."

Matthew 9:36, KJV

"O Jerusalem, Jerusalem, thou that killest the prophets, and stonest them which are sent unto thee, how often would I have gathered thy children together, even as a hen gathereth her chickens under her wings, and ye would not!"

Matthew 23:37, KJV

"Greater love hath no man than this, that a man lay down his life for his friends."

John 15:13, KJV

"But God commendeth his love toward us, in that, while we were yet sinners, Christ died for us."

Romans 5:8, KJV

"But God, who is rich in mercy, for his great love wherewith he loved us,

"Even when we were dead in sins, hath quickened us together with Christ, (by grace ye are saved;)

"And hath raised us up together, and made us sit together in heavenly places in Christ Jesus:

"That in the ages to come he might shew the exceeding riches of his grace in his kindness toward us through Christ Jesus."

Ephesians 2:4-7, KJV

3.

For God so loved the world

"For all have sinned, and come short of the glory of God;"

Romans 3:23, KJV

"And this is the condemnation, that light is come into the world, and men loved darkness rather than light, because their deeds were evil."

John 3:19, KJV

"All we like sheep have gone astray; we have turned every one to his own way; and the LORD hath laid on him the iniquity of us all."

Isaiah 53:6, KJV

"Behold, I was shapen in iniquity; and in sin did my mother conceive me."

Psalms 51:5, KJV

"And unto Adam he said, Because thou hast hearkened unto the voice of thy wife, and hast eaten of the tree, of which I commanded thee, saying, Thou shalt not eat of it: cursed is the ground for thy sake; in sorrow shalt thou eat of it all the days of thy life;

"Thorns also and thistles shall it bring forth to thee; and thou shalt eat the herb of the field;

For God so loved **the world...**

(cont.) "In the sweat of thy face shalt thou eat bread, till thou return unto the ground; for out of it wast thou taken: for dust thou art, and unto dust shalt thou return."

Genesis 3:17-19, KJV

"Wherefore, as by one man sin entered into the world, and death by sin; and so death passed upon all men, for that all have sinned:"

Romans 5:12, KJV

"And GOD saw that the wickedness of man was great in the earth, and that every imagination of the thoughts of his heart was only evil continually."

Genesis 6:5, KJV

"The heart is deceitful above all things, and desperately wicked: who can know it?"

Jeremiah 17:9, KJV

"Because that, when they knew God, they glorified him not as God, neither were thankful; but became vain in their imaginations, and their foolish heart was darkened.

"Professing themselves to be wise, they became fools,

"And changed the glory of the uncorruptible God into an image made like to corruptible man, and to birds, and fourfooted beasts, and creeping things.

For God so loved **the world…**

(cont.) "Wherefore God also gave them up to uncleanness through the lusts of their own hearts, to dishonour their own bodies between themselves:

"Who changed the truth of God into a lie, and worshipped and served the creature more than the Creator, who is blessed for ever. Amen."

Romans 1:21-25, KJV

"For when we were yet without strength, in due time Christ died for the ungodly.

"For scarcely for a righteous man will one die: yet peradventure for a good man some would even dare to die.

"But God commendeth his love toward us, in that, while we were yet sinners, Christ died for us."

Romans 5:6-8, KJV

4.

For God so loved the world, that he gave

"For unto us a child is born, unto us a son is given: and the government shall be upon his shoulder: and his name shall be called Wonderful, Counsellor, The mighty God, The everlasting Father, The Prince of Peace."

Isaiah 9:6, KJV

"But when the fulness of the time was come, God sent forth his Son, made of a woman, made under the law,"

Galatians 4:4, KJV

"And the angel said unto her, Fear not, Mary: for thou hast found favour with God.

"And, behold, thou shalt conceive in thy womb, and bring forth a son, and shalt call his name JESUS.

"He shall be great, and shall be called the Son of the Highest: and the Lord God shall give unto him the throne of his father David:

"And he shall reign over the house of Jacob for ever; and of his kingdom there shall be no end.

"Then said Mary unto the angel, How shall this be, seeing I know not a man?

For God so loved the world, **that he gave...**

(cont.) "And the angel answered and said unto her, The Holy Ghost shall come upon thee, and the power of the Highest shall overshadow thee: therefore also that holy thing which shall be born of thee shall be called the Son of God."

Luke 1:30-35

"Herein is love, not that we loved God, but that he loved us, and sent his Son to be the propitiation for our sins."

1 John 4:10, KJV

"And, lo, the angel of the Lord came upon them, and the glory of the Lord shone round about them: and they were sore afraid.

"And the angel said unto them, Fear not: for, behold, I bring you good tidings of great joy, which shall be to all people.

"For unto you is born this day in the city of David a Saviour, which is Christ the Lord."

Luke 2:9-11, KJV

"And we have seen and do testify that the Father sent the Son to be the Saviour of the world."

1 John 4:14, KJV

"Jesus answered and said unto them, This is the work of God, that ye believe on him whom he hath sent."

John 6:29, KJV

For God so loved the world, **that he gave...**

"For even the Son of man came not to be ministered unto, but to minister, and to give his life a ransom for many."

Mark 10:45, KJV

"Yet it pleased the LORD to bruise him; he hath put him to grief: when thou shalt make his soul an offering for sin, he shall see his seed, he shall prolong his days, and the pleasure of the LORD shall prosper in his hand.

Isaiah 53:10, KJV

"Who was delivered for our offences, and was raised again for our justification."

Romans 4:25, KJV

5.

For God so loved the world, that
he gave his only begotten Son

"For unto us a child is born, unto us a son is given: and the government shall be upon his shoulder: and his name shall be called Wonderful, Counsellor, The mighty God, The everlasting Father, The Prince of Peace."

Isaiah 9:6, KJV

"For this purpose the Son of God was manifested, that he might destroy the works of the devil."

1 John 3:8b, KJV

"I will declare the decree: the LORD hath said unto me, Thou art my Son; this day have I begotten thee."

Psalms 2:7, KJV (Hebrews 1:5, KJV)

"For the Son of man is come to seek and to save that which was lost."

Luke 19:10, KJV

For God so loved the world, that he gave **his only begotten son…**

"God, who at sundry times and in divers manners spake in time past unto the fathers by the prophets,

"Hath in these last days spoken unto us by his Son, whom he hath appointed heir of all things, by whom also he made the worlds;"

Hebrews 1:1-2, KJV

"For unto which of the angels said he at any time, Thou art my Son, this day have I begotten thee? And again, I will be to him a Father, and he shall be to me a Son?"

Hebrews 1:5, KJV

"For he shall grow up before him as a tender plant, and as a root out of a dry ground: he hath no form nor comeliness; and when we shall see him, there is no beauty that we should desire him.

"He is despised and rejected of men; a man of sorrows, and acquainted with grief: and we hid as it were our faces from him; he was despised, and we esteemed him not.

"Surely he hath borne our griefs, and carried our sorrows: yet we did esteem him stricken, smitten of God, and afflicted.

"But he was wounded for our transgressions, he was bruised for our iniquities: the chastisement of our peace was upon him; and with his stripes we are healed.

"All we like sheep have gone astray; we have turned every one to his own way; and the LORD hath laid on him the iniquity of us all.

"He was oppressed, and he was afflicted, yet he opened not his mouth: he is brought as a lamb to the slaughter, and as a sheep before her shearers is dumb, so he openeth not his mouth.

For God so loved the world, that he gave **his only begotten son...**

(cont.) "He was taken from prison and from judgment: and who shall declare his generation? for he was cut off out of the land of the living: for the transgression of my people was he stricken.

"And he made his grave with the wicked, and with the rich in his death; because he had done no violence, neither was any deceit in his mouth.

"Yet it pleased the LORD to bruise him; he hath put him to grief: when thou shalt make his soul an offering for sin, he shall see his seed, he shall prolong his days, and the pleasure of the LORD shall prosper in his hand.

"He shall see of the travail of his soul, and shall be satisfied: by his knowledge shall my righteous servant justify many; for he shall bear their iniquities.

"Therefore will I divide him a portion with the great, and he shall divide the spoil with the strong; because he hath poured out his soul unto death: and he was numbered with the transgressors; and he bare the sin of many, and made intercession for the transgressors."

Isaiah 53:2-12, KJV

"For in him dwelleth all the fulness of the Godhead bodily."

Colossians 2:9, KJV

"Jesus Christ the same yesterday, and to day, and for ever."

Hebrews 13:8, KJV

For God so loved the world, that he gave **his only begotten son…**

"But he held his peace, and answered nothing. Again the high priest asked him, and said unto him, Art thou the Christ, the Son of the Blessed?

"And Jesus said, I am: and ye shall see the Son of man sitting on the right hand of power, and coming in the clouds of heaven."

Mark 14:61-62, KJV

"For verily he took not on him the nature of angels; but he took on him the seed of Abraham.

"Wherefore in all things it behoved him to be made like unto his brethren, that he might be a merciful and faithful high priest in things pertaining to God, to make reconciliation for the sins of the people."

Hebrews 2:16-17, KJV

"And the Word was made flesh, and dwelt among us, (and we beheld his glory, the glory as of the only begotten of the Father,) full of grace and truth."

John 1:14, KJV

"No man hath seen God at any time; the only begotten Son, which is in the bosom of the Father, he hath declared him."

John 1:18, KJV

For God so loved the world, that he gave **his only begotten son...**

"Think not that I am come to destroy the law, or the prophets: I am not come to destroy, but to fulfil."

Matthew 5:17, KJV

"But when the fulness of the time was come, God sent forth his Son, made of a woman, made under the law,"

Galatians 4:4, KJV

"And Moses verily was faithful in all his house, as a servant, for a testimony of those things which were to be spoken after;

"But Christ as a son over his own house; whose house are we, if we hold fast the confidence and the rejoicing of the hope firm unto the end.

Hebrews 3:5-6, KJV

"For the law was given by Moses, but grace and truth came by Jesus Christ."

John 1:17, KJV

"All things are delivered unto me of my Father: and no man knoweth the Son, but the Father; neither knoweth any man the Father, save the Son, and he to whomsoever the Son will reveal him."

Matthew 11:27, KJV

For God so loved the world, that he gave **his only begotten son...**

"Jesus saith unto him, I am the way, the truth, and the life: no man cometh unto the Father, but by me."

John 14:6, KJV

"The LORD hath sworn, and will not repent, Thou art a priest for ever after the order of Melchizedek."

Psalms 110:4, KJV

"Wherefore, holy brethren, partakers of the heavenly calling, consider the Apostle and High Priest of our profession, Christ Jesus;"

Hebrews 3:1, KJV

"But this man, because he continueth ever, hath an unchangeable priesthood.

"Wherefore he is able also to save them to the uttermost that come unto God by him, seeing he ever liveth to make intercession for them.

"For such an high priest became us, who is holy, harmless, undefiled, separate from sinners, and made higher than the heavens;

"Who needeth not daily, as those high priests, to offer up sacrifice, first for his own sins, and then for the people's: for this he did once, when he offered up himself.

"For the law maketh men high priests which have infirmity; but the word of the oath, which was since the law, maketh the Son, who is consecrated for evermore."

Hebrews 7:24-28, KJV

For God so loved the world, that he gave **his only begotten son…**

"Seeing then that we have a great high priest, that is passed into the heavens, Jesus the Son of God, let us hold fast our profession.

"For we have not an high priest which cannot be touched with the feeling of our infirmities; but was in all points tempted like as we are, yet without sin."

Hebrews 4:14-15, KJV

"Hear another parable: There was a certain householder, which planted a vineyard, and hedged it round about, and digged a winepress in it, and built a tower, and let it out to husbandmen, and went into a far country:

"And when the time of the fruit drew near, he sent his servants to the husbandmen, that they might receive the fruits of it.

"And the husbandmen took his servants, and beat one, and killed another, and stoned another.

"Again, he sent other servants more than the first: and they did unto them likewise.

"But last of all he sent unto them his son, saying, They will reverence my son.

"But when the husbandmen saw the son, they said among themselves, This is the heir; come, let us kill him, and let us seize on his inheritance.

"And they caught him, and cast him out of the vineyard, and slew him.

"When the lord therefore of the vineyard cometh, what will he do unto those husbandmen?

"They say unto him, He will miserably destroy those wicked men, and will let out his vineyard unto other husbandmen, which shall render him the fruits in their seasons.

For God so loved the world, that he gave **his only begotten son…**

(cont.) "Jesus saith unto them, Did ye never read in the scriptures, The stone which the builders rejected, the same is become the head of the corner: this is the Lord's doing, and it is marvellous in our eyes?

"Therefore say I unto you, The kingdom of God shall be taken from you, and given to a nation bringing forth the fruits thereof.

"And whosoever shall fall on this stone shall be broken: but on whomsoever it shall fall, it will grind him to powder.

Matthew 21:33-44, KJV

"That all men should honour the Son, even as they honour the Father. He that honoureth not the Son honoureth not the Father which hath sent him."

John 5:23, KJV

"Then Pilate entered into the judgment hall again, and called Jesus, and said unto him, Art thou the King of the Jews?

"Jesus answered him, Sayest thou this thing of thyself, or did others tell it thee of me?

"Pilate answered, Am I a Jew? Thine own nation and the chief priests have delivered thee unto me: what hast thou done?

"Jesus answered, My kingdom is not of this world: if my kingdom were of this world, then would my servants fight, that I should not be delivered to the Jews: but now is my kingdom not from hence.

"Pilate therefore said unto him, Art thou a king then? Jesus answered, Thou sayest that I am a king. To this end was I born, and for this cause came I into the world, that I should bear witness unto the truth. Every one that is of the truth heareth my voice.

For God so loved the world, that he gave **his only begotten son...**

(cont.) "Pilate saith unto him, What is truth? And when he had said this, he went out again unto the Jews, and saith unto them, I find in him no fault at all."

John 18:33-38, KJV

"Who, being in the form of God, thought it not robbery to be equal with God:

"But made himself of no reputation, and took upon him the form of a servant, and was made in the likeness of men:

"And being found in fashion as a man, he humbled himself, and became obedient unto death, even the death of the cross.

"Wherefore God also hath highly exalted him, and given him a name which is above every name:

"That at the name of Jesus every knee should bow, of things in heaven, and things in earth, and things under the earth;

"And that every tongue should confess that Jesus Christ is Lord, to the glory of God the Father."

Philippians 2:6-11, KJV

"The next day John seeth Jesus coming unto him, and saith, Behold the Lamb of God, which taketh away the sin of the world."

John 1:29, KJV

For God so loved the world, that he gave **his only begotten son…**

"Speak ye unto all the congregation of Israel, saying, In the tenth day of this month they shall take to them every man a lamb, according to the house of their fathers, a lamb for an house:

"And if the household be too little for the lamb, let him and his neighbour next unto his house take it according to the number of the souls; every man according to his eating shall make your count for the lamb.

"Your lamb shall be without blemish, a male of the first year: ye shall take it out from the sheep, or from the goats:

"And ye shall keep it up until the fourteenth day of the same month: and the whole assembly of the congregation of Israel shall kill it in the evening.

"And they shall take of the blood, and strike it on the two side posts and on the upper door post of the houses, wherein they shall eat it.

"And they shall eat the flesh in that night, roast with fire, and unleavened bread; and with bitter herbs they shall eat it.

"Eat not of it raw, nor sodden at all with water, but roast with fire; his head with his legs, and with the purtenance thereof.

"And ye shall let nothing of it remain until the morning; and that which remaineth of it until the morning ye shall burn with fire.

"And thus shall ye eat it; with your loins girded, your shoes on your feet, and your staff in your hand; and ye shall eat it in haste: it is the LORD'S passover.

"For I will pass through the land of Egypt this night, and will smite all the firstborn in the land of Egypt, both man and beast; and against all the gods of Egypt I will execute judgment: I am the LORD.

For God so loved the world, that he gave **his only begotten son...**

(cont.) "And the blood shall be to you for a token upon the houses where ye are: and when I see the blood, I will pass over you, and the plague shall not be upon you to destroy you, when I smite the land of Egypt."

Exodus 12:3-13, KJV

"And it was the third hour, and they crucified him.

"And the superscription of his accusation was written over, THE KING OF THE JEWS."

Mark 15:25-26, KJV

"And when the sabbath was past, Mary Magdalene, and Mary the mother of James, and Salome, had bought sweet spices, that they might come and anoint him.

"And very early in the morning the first day of the week, they came unto the sepulchre at the rising of the sun.

"And they said among themselves, Who shall roll us away the stone from the door of the sepulchre?

"And when they looked, they saw that the stone was rolled away: for it was very great.

"And entering into the sepulchre, they saw a young man sitting on the right side, clothed in a long white garment; and they were affrighted.

"And he saith unto them, Be not affrighted: Ye seek Jesus of Nazareth, which was crucified: he is risen; he is not here: behold the place where they laid him."

Mark 16:1-6, KJV

For God so loved the world, that he gave **his only begotten son…**

"(A Psalm of David.) The LORD said unto my Lord, Sit thou at my right hand, until I make thine enemies thy footstool."

Psalms 110:1, KJV

"Not every one that saith unto me, Lord, Lord, shall enter into the kingdom of heaven; but he that doeth the will of my Father which is in heaven.

"Many will say to me in that day, Lord, Lord, have we not prophesied in thy name? and in thy name have cast out devils? and in thy name done many wonderful works?

"And then will I profess unto them, I never knew you: depart from me, ye that work iniquity.

"Therefore whosoever heareth these sayings of mine, and doeth them, I will liken him unto a wise man, which built his house upon a rock:

"And the rain descended, and the floods came, and the winds blew, and beat upon that house; and it fell not: for it was founded upon a rock.

"And every one that heareth these sayings of mine, and doeth them not, shall be likened unto a foolish man, which built his house upon the sand:

"And the rain descended, and the floods came, and the winds blew, and beat upon that house; and it fell: and great was the fall of it.

"And it came to pass, when Jesus had ended these sayings, the people were astonished at his doctrine:

"For he taught them as one having authority, and not as the scribes."

Matthew 5:21-29, KJV

For God so loved the world, that he gave **his only begotten son…**

"The former treatise have I made, O Theophilus, of all that Jesus began both to do and teach,

"Until the day in which he was taken up, after that he through the Holy Ghost had given commandments unto the apostles whom he had chosen:

"To whom also he shewed himself alive after his passion by many infallible proofs, being seen of them forty days, and speaking of the things pertaining to the kingdom of God:

"And, being assembled together with them, commanded them that they should not depart from Jerusalem, but wait for the promise of the Father, which, saith he, ye have heard of me.

"For John truly baptized with water; but ye shall be baptized with the Holy Ghost not many days hence.

"….And he said unto them, It is not for you to know the times or the seasons, which the Father hath put in his own power.

"But ye shall receive power, after that the Holy Ghost is come upon you: and ye shall be witnesses unto me both in Jerusalem, and in all Judaea, and in Samaria, and unto the uttermost part of the earth.

"And when he had spoken these things, while they beheld, he was taken up; and a cloud received him out of their sight.

"And while they looked stedfastly toward heaven as he went up, behold, two men stood by them in white apparel;

"Which also said, Ye men of Galilee, why stand ye gazing up into heaven? this same Jesus, which is taken up from you into heaven, shall so come in like manner as ye have seen him go into heaven."

Acts 1-5, 7-11, KJV

For God so loved the world, that he gave **his only begotten son…**

"And he was clothed with a vesture dipped in blood: and his name is called The Word of God.

"And the armies which were in heaven followed him upon white horses, clothed in fine linen, white and clean.

"And out of his mouth goeth a sharp sword, that with it he should smite the nations: and he shall rule them with a rod of iron: and he treadeth the winepress of the fierceness and wrath of Almighty God.

"And he hath on his vesture and on his thigh a name written, KING OF KINGS, AND LORD OF LORDS."

Revelation 19:13-16, KJV

"And when all things shall be subdued unto him, then shall the Son also himself be subject unto him that put all things under him, that God may be all in all."

1 Corinthians 15:28, KJV

6.

For God so loved the world, that he gave his only begotten Son, that whosoever believeth in him

"Who hath believed our report? and to whom is the arm of the LORD revealed?"

Isaiah 53:1, KJV

"Jesus answered and said unto them, This is the work of God, that ye believe on him whom he hath sent."

John 6:29, KJV

"For by grace are ye saved through faith; and that not of yourselves: it is the gift of God:

Not of works, lest any man should boast."

Ephesians 2:8-9, KJV

"And he believed in the LORD; and he counted it to him for righteousness."

Genesis 15:6, KJV

For God so loved the world, that he gave his only begotten Son,

that **whosoever believeth in him…**

"And therefore it was imputed to him for righteousness.

"Now it was not written for his sake alone, that it was imputed to him;

"But for us also, to whom it shall be imputed, if we believe on him that raised up Jesus our Lord from the dead;"

Romans 4:22-24, KJV

"But without faith it is impossible to please him: for he that cometh to God must believe that he is, and that he is a rewarder of them that diligently seek him."

Hebrews 11:6, KJV

"Then Peter said unto them, Repent, and be baptized every one of you in the name of Jesus Christ for the remission of sins, and ye shall receive the gift of the Holy Ghost. For the promise is unto you, and to your children, and to all that are afar off, even as many as the Lord our God shall call. And with many other words did he testify and exhort, saying, Save yourselves from this untoward generation."

Acts 2:38-40, KJV

"Therefore being justified by faith, we have peace with God through our Lord Jesus Christ:

By whom also we have access by faith into this grace wherein we stand, and rejoice in hope of the glory of God."

Romans 5:1-2, KJV

For God so loved the world, that he gave his only begotten Son,

that **whosoever believeth in him…**

"Whosoever shall confess that Jesus is the Son of God, God dwelleth in him, and he in God."

1 John 4:15, KJV

"Whosoever believeth that Jesus is the Christ is born of God: and every one that loveth him that begat loveth him also that is begotten of him.

"By this we know that we love the children of God, when we love God, and keep his commandments.

"For this is the love of God, that we keep his commandments: and his commandments are not grievous.

"For whatsoever is born of God overcometh the world: and this is the victory that overcometh the world, even our faith.

"Who is he that overcometh the world, but he that believeth that Jesus is the Son of God?"

1 John 5:1-5, KJV

"Blessed is the man that trusteth in the LORD, and whose hope the LORD is.

"For he shall be as a tree planted by the waters, and that spreadeth out her roots by the river, and shall not see when heat cometh, but her leaf shall be green; and shall not be careful in the year of drought, neither shall cease from yielding fruit."

Jeremiah 17:7-8, KJV

For God so loved the world, that he gave his only begotten Son,

that **whosoever believeth in him…**

"Let not your heart be troubled: ye believe in God, believe also in me."

John 14:1, KJV

"Being justified freely by his grace through the redemption that is in Christ Jesus:

"Whom God hath set forth to be a propitiation through faith in his blood, to declare his righteousness for the remission of sins that are past, through the forbearance of God;

"To declare, I say, at this time his righteousness: that he might be just, and the justifier of him which believeth in Jesus."

Romans 3:24-26, KJV

"And as he passed by, he saw Levi the son of Alphaeus sitting at the receipt of custom, and said unto him, Follow me. And he arose and followed him."

Mark 2:14, KJV

"And when he had called the people unto him with his disciples also, he said unto them, Whosoever will come after me, let him deny himself, and take up his cross, and follow me."

Mark 8:34, KJV

For God so loved the world, that he gave his only begotten Son,

that **whosoever believeth in him...**

"Behold, the days come, saith the LORD, that I will make a new covenant with the house of Israel, and with the house of Judah:

"Not according to the covenant that I made with their fathers in the day that I took them by the hand to bring them out of the land of Egypt; which my covenant they brake, although I was an husband unto them, saith the LORD:

"But this shall be the covenant that I will make with the house of Israel; After those days, saith the LORD, I will put my law in their inward parts, and write it in their hearts; and will be their God, and they shall be my people.

"And they shall teach no more every man his neighbour, and every man his brother, saying, Know the LORD: for they shall all know me, from the least of them unto the greatest of them, saith the LORD: for I will forgive their iniquity, and I will remember their sin no more.

Jeremiah 31:31-34, KJV

"But as many as received him, to them gave he power to become the sons of God, even to them that believe on his name:"

John 1:12, KJV

"And brought them out, and said, Sirs, what must I do to be saved?

"And they said, Believe on the Lord Jesus Christ, and thou shalt be saved, and thy house.

"And they spake unto him the word of the Lord, and to all that were in his house.

For God so loved the world, that he gave his only begotten Son,

that **whosoever believeth in him…**

(cont.) "And he took them the same hour of the night, and washed their stripes; and was baptized, he and all his, straightway.

"And when he had brought them into his house, he set meat before them, and rejoiced, believing in God with all his house."

Acts 16:30-34, KJV

"Be it known unto you all, and to all the people of Israel, that by the name of Jesus Christ of Nazareth, whom ye crucified, whom God raised from the dead, even by him doth this man stand here before you whole.

"This is the stone which was set at nought of you builders, which is become the head of the corner.

"Neither is there salvation in any other: for there is none other name under heaven given among men, whereby we must be saved."

Acts 4:11-12, KJV

"But we are not of them who draw back unto perdition; but of them that believe to the saving of the soul."

Hebrews 10:39, KJV

7.

For God so loved the world, that he gave his only begotten Son, that whosoever believeth in him should not perish

"Then said one unto him, Lord, are there few that be saved? And he said unto them,

"Strive to enter in at the strait gate: for many, I say unto you, will seek to enter in, and shall not be able.

"When once the master of the house is risen up, and hath shut to the door, and ye begin to stand without, and to knock at the door, saying, Lord, Lord, open unto us; and he shall answer and say unto you, I know you not whence ye are:

"Then shall ye begin to say, We have eaten and drunk in thy presence, and thou hast taught in our streets.

"But he shall say, I tell you, I know you not whence ye are; depart from me, all ye workers of iniquity.

"There shall be weeping and gnashing of teeth, when ye shall see Abraham, and Isaac, and Jacob, and all the prophets, in the kingdom of God, and you yourselves thrust out.

Luke 13:23-28, KJV

"Again, the kingdom of heaven is like unto a net, that was cast into the sea, and gathered of every kind:

"Which, when it was full, they drew to shore, and sat down, and gathered the good into vessels, but cast the bad away.

For God so loved the world, that he gave his only begotten Son, that whosoever believeth in him **should not perish...**

(cont.) "So shall it be at the end of the world: the angels shall come forth, and sever the wicked from among the just,

"And shall cast them into the furnace of fire: there shall be wailing and gnashing of teeth."

Matthew 13:47-50, KJV

"Another parable put he forth unto them, saying, The kingdom of heaven is likened unto a man which sowed good seed in his field:

"But while men slept, his enemy came and sowed tares among the wheat, and went his way.

"But when the blade was sprung up, and brought forth fruit, then appeared the tares also.

"So the servants of the householder came and said unto him, Sir, didst not thou sow good seed in thy field? from whence then hath it tares?

"He said unto them, An enemy hath done this. The servants said unto him, Wilt thou then that we go and gather them up?

"But he said, Nay; lest while ye gather up the tares, ye root up also the wheat with them.

"Let both grow together until the harvest: and in the time of harvest I will say to the reapers, Gather ye together first the tares, and bind them in bundles to burn them: but gather the wheat into my barn...."

"Then Jesus sent the multitude away, and went into the house: and his disciples came unto him, saying, Declare unto us the parable of the tares of the field.

"He answered and said unto them, He that soweth the good seed is the Son of man;

For God so loved the world, that he gave his only begotten Son, that whosoever believeth in him **should not perish…**

(cont.) "The field is the world; the good seed are the children of the kingdom; but the tares are the children of the wicked one;

"The enemy that sowed them is the devil; the harvest is the end of the world; and the reapers are the angels.

"As therefore the tares are gathered and burned in the fire; so shall it be in the end of this world.

"The Son of man shall send forth his angels, and they shall gather out of his kingdom all things that offend, and them which do iniquity;

"And shall cast them into a furnace of fire: there shall be wailing and gnashing of teeth.

"Then shall the righteous shine forth as the sun in the kingdom of their Father. Who hath ears to hear, let him hear."

Matthew 13:24-30; 36-43

"There was a certain rich man, which was clothed in purple and fine linen, and fared sumptuously every day:

"And there was a certain beggar named Lazarus, which was laid at his gate, full of sores,

"And desiring to be fed with the crumbs which fell from the rich man's table: moreover the dogs came and licked his sores.

"And it came to pass, that the beggar died, and was carried by the angels into Abraham's bosom: the rich man also died, and was buried;

"And in hell he lift up his eyes, being in torments, and seeth Abraham afar off, and Lazarus in his bosom.

For God so loved the world, that he gave his only begotten Son, that whosoever believeth in him **should not perish...**

(cont.) "And he cried and said, Father Abraham, have mercy on me, and send Lazarus, that he may dip the tip of his finger in water, and cool my tongue; for I am tormented in this flame.

"But Abraham said, Son, remember that thou in thy lifetime receivedst thy good things, and likewise Lazarus evil things: but now he is comforted, and thou art tormented.

"And beside all this, between us and you there is a great gulf fixed: so that they which would pass from hence to you cannot; neither can they pass to us, that would come from thence."

Luke 16:19-26, KJV

"And they shall go forth, and look upon the carcases of the men that have transgressed against me: for their worm shall not die, neither shall their fire be quenched; and they shall be an abhorring unto all flesh."

Isaiah 66:24, KJV

"And you hath he quickened, who were dead in trespasses and sins;"

Ephesians 2:1, KJV

"But and if that evil servant shall say in his heart, My lord delayeth his coming;

"And shall begin to smite his fellowservants, and to eat and drink with the drunken;

"The lord of that servant shall come in a day when he looketh not for him, and in an hour that he is not aware of,

For God so loved the world, that he gave his only begotten Son, that whosoever believeth in him **should not perish…**

(cont.) "And shall cut him asunder, and appoint him his portion with the hypocrites: there shall be weeping and gnashing of teeth."

Matthew 24: 48-51, KJV

"For God sent not his Son into the world to condemn the world; but that the world through him might be saved.

"He that believeth on him is not condemned: but he that believeth not is condemned already, because he hath not believed in the name of the only begotten Son of God.

"And this is the condemnation, that light is come into the world, and men loved darkness rather than light, because their deeds were evil.

"For every one that doeth evil hateth the light, neither cometh to the light, lest his deeds should be reproved."

John 3:17-20, KJV

"And I say unto you, That many shall come from the east and west, and shall sit down with Abraham, and Isaac, and Jacob, in the kingdom of heaven.

But the children of the kingdom shall be cast out into outer darkness: there shall be weeping and gnashing of teeth."

Matthew 8:11-12, KJV

For God so loved the world, that he gave his only begotten Son, that whosoever believeth in him **should not perish…**

"So those servants went out into the highways, and gathered together all as many as they found, both bad and good: and the wedding was furnished with guests.

"And when the king came in to see the guests, he saw there a man which had not on a wedding garment:

"And he saith unto him, Friend, how camest thou in hither not having a wedding garment? And he was speechless.

"Then said the king to the servants, Bind him hand and foot, and take him away, and cast him into outer darkness; there shall be weeping and gnashing of teeth.

"For many are called, but few are chosen."

Matthew 22:10-14, KJV

"When the Son of man shall come in his glory, and all the holy angels with him, then shall he sit upon the throne of his glory:

"And before him shall be gathered all nations: and he shall separate them one from another, as a shepherd divideth his sheep from the goats….

"Then shall he say also unto them on the left hand, Depart from me, ye cursed, into everlasting fire, prepared for the devil and his angels:

"For I was an hungred, and ye gave me no meat: I was thirsty, and ye gave me no drink:

"I was a stranger, and ye took me not in: naked, and ye clothed me not: sick, and in prison, and ye visited me not.

"Then shall they also answer him, saying, Lord, when saw we thee an hungred, or athirst, or a stranger, or naked, or sick, or in prison, and did not minister unto thee?

For God so loved the world, that he gave his only begotten Son, that whosoever believeth in him **should not perish…**

(cont.) Then shall he answer them, saying, Verily I say unto you, Inasmuch as ye did it not to one of the least of these, ye did it not to me.

"And these shall go away into everlasting punishment: but the righteous into life eternal."

Matthew 25:31-32, 41-46

"And I saw a great white throne, and him that sat on it, from whose face the earth and the heaven fled away; and there was found no place for them.

"And I saw the dead, small and great, stand before God; and the books were opened: and another book was opened, which is the book of life: and the dead were judged out of those things which were written in the books, according to their works.

"And the sea gave up the dead which were in it; and death and hell delivered up the dead which were in them: and they were judged every man according to their works.

"And death and hell were cast into the lake of fire. This is the second death.

"And whosoever was not found written in the book of life was cast into the lake of fire."

Revelation 20:11-15, KJV

For God so loved the world, that he gave his only begotten Son, that whosoever believeth in him **should not perish...**

"But the fearful, and unbelieving, and the abominable, and murderers, and whoremongers, and sorcerers, and idolaters, and all liars, shall have their part in the lake which burneth with fire and brimstone: which is the second death."

Revelation 21:8, KJV

"And there shall in no wise enter into it any thing that defileth, neither whatsoever worketh abomination, or maketh a lie: but they which are written in the Lamb's book of life."

Revelation 21:27, KJV

"For unto every one that hath shall be given, and he shall have abundance: but from him that hath not shall be taken away even that which he hath.

"And cast ye the unprofitable servant into outer darkness: there shall be weeping and gnashing of teeth."

Matthew 25:29-30, KJV

"There shall be weeping and gnashing of teeth, when ye shall see Abraham, and Isaac, and Jacob, and all the prophets, in the kingdom of God, and you yourselves thrust out."

Luke 13:28, KJV

For God so loved the world, that he gave his only begotten Son, that whosoever believeth in him **should not perish…**

"And the LORD God commanded the man, saying, Of every tree of the garden thou mayest freely eat:

"But of the tree of the knowledge of good and evil, thou shalt not eat of it: for in the day that thou eatest thereof thou shalt surely die."

Genesis 2:16-17, KJV

"Wherefore, as by one man sin entered into the world, and death by sin; and so death passed upon all men, for that all have sinned:"

Romans 5:12, KJV

"For the wages of sin is death; but the gift of God is eternal life through Jesus Christ our Lord."

Romans 6:23, KJV

8.

For God so loved the world, that he gave his only begotten Son, that whosoever believeth in him should not perish, but have everlasting life

"Jesus said unto her, I am the resurrection, and the life: he that believeth in me, though he were dead, yet shall he live:

"And whosoever liveth and believeth in me shall never die. Believest thou this?"

John 11:25-26, KJV

"And I saw a new heaven and a new earth: for the first heaven and the first earth were passed away; and there was no more sea.

"And I John saw the holy city, new Jerusalem, coming down from God out of heaven, prepared as a bride adorned for her husband.

"And I heard a great voice out of heaven saying, Behold, the tabernacle of God is with men, and he will dwell with them, and they shall be his people, and God himself shall be with them, and be their God.

"And God shall wipe away all tears from their eyes; and there shall be no more death, neither sorrow, nor crying, neither shall there be any more pain: for the former things are passed away.

"And he that sat upon the throne said, Behold, I make all things new. And he said unto me, Write: for these words are true and faithful.

"And he said unto me, It is done. I am Alpha and Omega, the beginning and the end. I will give unto him that is athirst of the fountain of the water of life freely.

For God so loved the world, that he gave his only begotten Son, that whosoever believeth in him should not perish, but **have everlasting life.**

(cont.) "He that overcometh shall inherit all things; and I will be his God, and he shall be my son."

Revelation 21:1-7, KJV

"Wherefore he is able also to save them to the uttermost that come unto God by him, seeing he ever liveth to make intercession for them."

Hebrews 7:25, KJV

"And I say unto you, That many shall come from the east and west, and shall sit down with Abraham, and Isaac, and Jacob, in the kingdom of heaven."

Matthew 8:11, KJV

"And this is the promise that he hath promised us, even eternal life."

1 John 2:25, KJV

"And this is the record, that God hath given to us eternal life, and this life is in his Son."

1 John 5:11, KJV

"In hope of eternal life, which God, that cannot lie, promised before the world began;"

Titus 1:2, KJV

For God so loved the world, that he gave his only begotten Son, that whosoever believeth in him should not perish, but **have everlasting life.**

"And Jesus answered and said, Verily I say unto you, There is no man that hath left house, or brethren, or sisters, or father, or mother, or wife, or children, or lands, for my sake, and the gospel's,

"But he shall receive an hundredfold now in this time, houses, and brethren, and sisters, and mothers, and children, and lands, with persecutions; and in the world to come eternal life."

Mark 10:29-30, KJV

"When the Son of man shall come in his glory, and all the holy angels with him, then shall he sit upon the throne of his glory:

"And before him shall be gathered all nations: and he shall separate them one from another, as a shepherd divideth his sheep from the goats:

"And he shall set the sheep on his right hand, but the goats on the left.

"Then shall the King say unto them on his right hand, Come, ye blessed of my Father, inherit the kingdom prepared for you from the foundation of the world:

"For I was an hungred, and ye gave me meat: I was thirsty, and ye gave me drink: I was a stranger, and ye took me in:

"Naked, and ye clothed me: I was sick, and ye visited me: I was in prison, and ye came unto me.

"Then shall the righteous answer him, saying, Lord, when saw we thee an hungred, and fed thee? or thirsty, and gave thee drink?

"When saw we thee a stranger, and took thee in? or naked, and clothed thee?

"Or when saw we thee sick, or in prison, and came unto thee?

For God so loved the world, that he gave his only begotten Son, that whosoever believeth in him should not perish, but **have everlasting life.**

(cont.) "And the King shall answer and say unto them, Verily I say unto you, Inasmuch as ye have done it unto one of the least of these my brethren, ye have done it unto me.

"Then shall he say also unto them on the left hand, Depart from me, ye cursed, into everlasting fire, prepared for the devil and his angels....

"And these shall go away into everlasting punishment: but the righteous into life eternal."

Matthew 25:31-41, 46, KJV

"And as touching the dead, that they rise: have ye not read in the book of Moses, how in the bush God spake unto him, saying, I am the God of Abraham, and the God of Isaac, and the God of Jacob?"

Mark 12:26, KJV

"And he shewed me a pure river of water of life, clear as crystal, proceeding out of the throne of God and of the Lamb.

"In the midst of the street of it, and on either side of the river, was there the tree of life, which bare twelve manner of fruits, and yielded her fruit every month: and the leaves of the tree were for the healing of the nations.

"And there shall be no more curse: but the throne of God and of the Lamb shall be in it; and his servants shall serve him:

"And they shall see his face; and his name shall be in their foreheads.

"And there shall be no night there; and they need no candle, neither light of the sun; for the Lord God giveth them light: and they shall reign for ever and ever."

Revelation 22:1-5, KJV

For God so loved the world, that he gave his only begotten Son, that whosoever believeth in him should not perish, but **have everlasting life.**

"And the city had no need of the sun, neither of the moon, to shine in it: for the glory of God did lighten it, and the Lamb is the light thereof.

"And the nations of them which are saved shall walk in the light of it: and the kings of the earth do bring their glory and honour into it.

"And the gates of it shall not be shut at all by day: for there shall be no night there.

"And they shall bring the glory and honour of the nations into it.

"And there shall in no wise enter into it any thing that defileth, neither whatsoever worketh abomination, or maketh a lie: but they which are written in the Lamb's book of life.

Revelation 21:23-27, KJV

"Keep yourselves in the love of God, looking for the mercy of our Lord Jesus Christ unto eternal life."

Jude 1:21, KJV

"For we know that if our earthly house of this tabernacle were dissolved, we have a building of God, an house not made with hands, eternal in the heavens."

2 Corinthians 5:1, KJV

"Neither by the blood of goats and calves, but by his own blood he entered in once into the holy place, having obtained eternal redemption for us."

Hebrews 9:12, KJV

For God so loved the world, that he gave his only begotten Son, that whosoever believeth in him should not perish, but **have everlasting life.**

"My sheep hear my voice, and I know them, and they follow me:

"And I give unto them eternal life; and they shall never perish, neither shall any man pluck them out of my hand."

John 10:27-28, KJV

"And I say unto you, That many shall come from the east and west, and shall sit down with Abraham, and Isaac, and Jacob, in the kingdom of heaven."

Matthew 8:11, KJV

"These words spake Jesus, and lifted up his eyes to heaven, and said, Father, the hour is come; glorify thy Son, that thy Son also may glorify thee:

"As thou hast given him power over all flesh, that he should give eternal life to as many as thou hast given him.

"And this is life eternal, that they might know thee the only true God, and Jesus Christ, whom thou hast sent."

John 17:1-3, KJV

"Neither pray I for these alone, but for them also which shall believe on me through their word;

"That they all may be one; as thou, Father, art in me, and I in thee, that they also may be one in us: that the world may believe that thou hast sent me.

For God so loved the world, that he gave his only begotten Son, that whosoever believeth in him should not perish, but **have everlasting life.**

(cont.) "And the glory which thou gavest me I have given them; that they may be one, even as we are one:

"I in them, and thou in me, that they may be made perfect in one; and that the world may know that thou hast sent me, and hast loved them, as thou hast loved me.

"Father, I will that they also, whom thou hast given me, be with me where I am; that they may behold my glory, which thou hast given me: for thou lovedst me before the foundation of the world."

John 17:20-24, KJV

"These things have I written unto you that believe on the name of the Son of God; that ye may know that ye have eternal life, and that ye may believe on the name of the Son of God."

1 John 5:13, KJV

Closing Remarks

There is nothing and no one more worth considering than the Lord our God. "Consider him," writes the author of the book of Hebrews. In considering Jesus and his teaching, we remember He taught that gaining vast wealth, even the whole world, will avail us nothing if we lose our souls. So we pause. We slow down and consider his direction to seek first the kingdom of God. We slow our reading and weigh each verse in Holy Scripture and its meaning, its author, its audience, its context, its purpose. To read Holy Scripture is to hear from God – if we have ears to hear. We meditate on Holy Scripture rather than fly over it to meet some arbitrary quota or check a box on a checklist.

Meditating on God brings us to contemplate the contrast between God and man. We read the words, "for God so loved the world," and we ask, well, so what? Is that supposed to be amazing? What's so surprising about that? The world seems like a pretty nice place filled with nice, decent, polite people. How can the truth in this verse mean anything to us if we do not first ask, seek, and discover who God is?

When Moses asked who He is, what his name is, He revealed Himself as the great I AM. Beside Him who is, we are not. He is infallible, and we are fallible. He is pure and perfect, and we are broken and in need of a redeemer. Praise the Lord that He sent us a Redeemer! We meditate on God. He is wise, and the wisest of us is foolish next to Him. He is the Creator, and we are created. Among the billions of souls on the planet, each of us is the tiniest pinprick of existence, and our lives are the tiniest speck in the history of humanity. Yet even all the years of humanity and all the years of this planet's existence from its creation to its end are the tiniest pinpricks of specks in the vast ocean of eternity. Even an ocean compared to a speck is not enough of a contrast because an ocean has its limits and eternity has none.

Meditating on God, words fail us. Our finite minds fail us. Just trying to grasp the concept of eternality stretches us past our limits – and then add in the fact that God has revealed Himself as immutable, and we are carried to a new level of understanding – or more accurately, a new level of understanding of how little we can understand. He created and yet was the same when He was creating as He was before creation. His plan and purpose for the world and for each of us little specks is unchanging because He does not change, which means there was never a moment (can there be "moments" in the vastness of eternity before the creation of time?) when God did not intend to create the universe and save souls for his glory.

What can we say? God is ineffable; there is everything to be said but only insufficient words and finite minds at our disposal. Nothing we can say begins to approach adequate description. He is holy, perfect, just, gracious, merciful, omnipotent, omniscient; He is light, and He is love. He is our glorious Father in heaven.

We meditate on God and begin to see that spending the rest of eternity with Him, praising Him, adoring Him, abiding with Him, is exceedingly abundantly more than we can hope for (and yet it is our hope!) and exceedingly abundantly more than we can fathom, and is the substance of the eternal life promised us by and through his only begotten son, Jesus Christ. It is a blessing to know that this eternal life we are promised has already begun for those who are saved. Eternal life is not a gift we'll receive someday; we have received it already. We are children of God now. Jesus promised, "whosoever liveth and believeth in me shall never die."

Teaching children has proved to be my calling. Only God knows whether any of the seeds we scatter will take root and produce a crop. As we teach, we are humbly mindful that the children of God are born not of blood or of the will of the flesh or the will of man but of God. As we teach children, the Lord teaches us. When I pray and ask the Lord what He wants me to say to the little ones, verses come to my mind, one after another, and along with those verses come other words I might use to explain those verses to children. Oftentimes, the best explanation, exposition and illustration of Scripture is Scripture. We want to know God, so we meditate on His word. We want to make God known to others, and having learned from Him, we are householders with a heap of treasures, new and old, in our treasure house – the Bible, filled with story after story showing how God deals with people and how He speaks with people. His word shows us who He is.

I hope this meditation is helpful to you personally as you contemplate our Creator, our Savior, our Lord. Even more than that, I hope this is helpful to you as you teach others about Christ Jesus and our Heavenly Father. As we have freely received, we freely give. Has the Lord shown you truth? Share it with someone. It is more blessed to give than to receive. We must work while it is day, for the night is coming when we will sleep.

May the grace of our Lord Jesus Christ, and the love of God, and the fellowship and communion of the Holy Spirit abide with us and lead us in our meditations on Him, now this day and for all eternity, Amen.

The Children's Teacher